MW00388837

Black Boy Soar

Written by: Dwight Johnson

Copyright information © 2019 Dwight Johnson, Black Boy Soar

All Rights Reserved. This book or any portion thereof may not be reproduced or used in any manner whatsoever without the express written permission of the publisher except for the use of brief quotations in the book review.

Printed in the United States of America
First Printing 2019

Black boy, black boy
You're beautiful in every shape.
Whether you're tall, short, with braids
or wear a fade.

Whether you run, skip, hop, or jump in play,
Your joy is evident, for all it should be displayed.

Black boy, black boy
There's nothing you can't do
Just imagine all that is out there waiting for you.

Lawyer, doctor, researcher, or teacher
Activist, athlete, barber, or preacher

Nurse, CEO, principal, or writer
Fireman, police officer, or even a skydiver
Artist, mechanic, college student, or a chef
Musician, dentist, or a vet.

All these things and more can be yours.
Black boy, black boy you can and will soar.

Black boy, black boy
Don't get me wrong, please.
The world is yours, but it won't come with ease.

Nothing will be given or handed or shared.
You will have to give it all you got with every piece
of fight you can bare.
Will it be hard? Will it challenge you?
You can bet it will!
But the reward of being all you can be will make it
worth it even still.

Black boy, black boy
You are a king no doubt.
Full of creativity, wisdom, goodness, someone the
world needs to know about.

You are valued, loved, seen, and treasured
Everything you are reflects the best of God, your
Father in Heaven.

Black boy, black boy
You're unstoppable indeed.
You have all it takes in this world to succeed.

In you, there is a power, a strength you possess,
To be and do all you desire, to be the absolute best.

Never take a "no" as the end of your story, as if
you can't win you see,
Because black boy, black boy
A winner is what you are and what you will always be.

About the author:

Dwight Johnson has dedicated the last decade to ministry to youth and their families in both Mississippi and now Nashville, Tennessee where he serves as the Director of Youth at Preston Taylor Ministries in West Nashville. Having served both in the local church and in parachurch organizations, Dwight loves working with kids and teenagers, specifically middle schoolers and enjoys seeing youth see their potential and reach their God-inspired dreams. In addition, Dwight travels throughout the south speaking at youth-retreats and leading workshops and conferences that helps other youth workers grow.

Contact Dwight:

Email: djinspiresyou@gmail.com
Instagram: @imdwightjohnson
Facebook: Dwight Johnson

31853207R00019

Made in the USA
Lexington, KY
25 February 2019